DISNEY · PIXAR

INSIDE OUT

THE JUNIOR NOVELIZATION

ISBN 978-0-7364-3312-9

randomhousekids.com

Printed in the United States of America

10 9 8 7 6 5 4

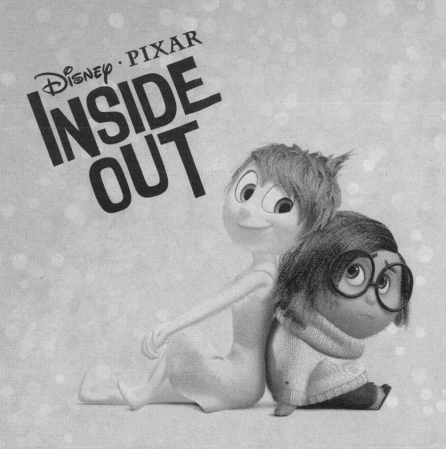

DISNEY · PIXAR
INSIDE OUT

THE JUNIOR NOVELIZATION

Adapted by Suzanne Francis

Random House 🏠 New York

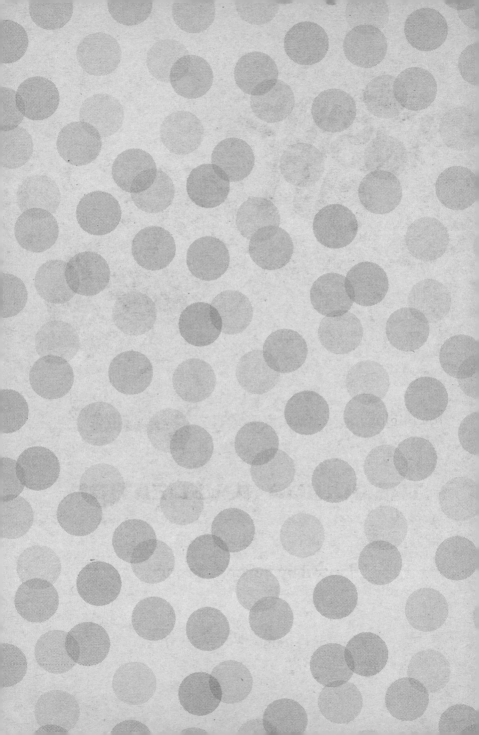

On the day Riley was born, Joy found herself inside a strange and beautiful place: Riley's mind. Joy, a glowing collection of yellow energy particles, was one of the new baby's Emotions. From inside Headquarters, the control center of Riley's Mind World, she saw everything through Riley's eyes.

Joy stepped up to the console, a device the Emotions used to control Riley's reactions, and watched in awe, as Riley's parents looked down at their beautiful daughter for the first time. "Hello, Riley," said Mom, beaming.

"Oh, look at you," said Dad in amazement. "Aren't

you a little bundle of joy."

Suddenly, a golden sphere rolled down a track to the right of the console in Headquarters, lighting up the room with its soft glow. Joy picked up the strange globe and held it carefully in her hands. She could see an image of Riley's parents, smiling inside the sphere. "Aren't you a little bundle of joy," said Dad. It was the memory of what Joy had just witnessed! She placed the memory sphere back and watched as it continued rolling down the track to the memory shelves in the back of Headquarters.

Joy instantly fell in love with Riley and devoted herself completely to doing everything she could to help Riley live a happy life. She thought it would just be her and Riley forever . . . But thirty-three seconds after Riley was born, someone else materialized at the console and started working the controls. Riley began to cry.

"I'm Sadness," the blue newcomer said to Joy, introducing herself somberly.

"I just want to fix that," Joy said, gently pushing Sadness off the controls. She pressed a few buttons and Riley stopped crying.

As time went on, more Emotions showed up inside

Headquarters, taking control whenever Riley needed them. And with each new Emotion, memories started rolling through in different colors, matching the Emotion that Riley felt about the memory.

Fear's job was to keep Riley safe. He guided her whenever she encountered something he thought was dangerous, like power cords, roller skates, and dogs. "Look out!" was one of his favorite phrases. All of Riley's memories associated with Fear were stored in purple spheres, the same color as Fear himself.

Disgust was green. She kept her sharp eye out for anything that looked worthy of an "Ew." She took control whenever something gross came up—like broccoli, bad art, or nasty people. Basically, Disgust kept Riley from being physically or socially poisoned. Riley's disgusted memories were saved inside green spheres.

When the Emotions saw unfair things happening to Riley as they watched out the view screen in Headquarters, Anger—who was short, red, and angry—took the reins. Life's injustices really heated him up! Anger worked hard to even the score, so he was always ready to release a scowl, scream, or growl at any unfair situation. When he got REALLY mad, he would get so hot that his head would light on fire! Riley's angry memories were saved inside red spheres.

Each Emotion had its own job, but most of the time they were content to let Joy run the console. And Joy could see why all of them were important . . . except for Sadness. Joy didn't want Riley to ever feel sad! She wanted Riley to be as happy as she could be, so she tried her best to keep Sadness as far from the controls as possible.

As Riley's lead Emotion, Joy did an excellent job, and most of Riley's memories were golden, just like Joy. The most important ones were core memories— these glowed brighter than Riley's normal memories. They were formed when Riley had big "life moments," like when she was two and a half and scored her first hockey goal in a game with her parents!

The core memories powered the Islands of Personality with lightlines, which were like electrical cords that stretched over a deep ravine from Headquarters to the actual islands. The islands made Riley who she was, and they each said something different about her. For example, the core memory of Riley's first goal powered Hockey Island. There were also Goofball, Family, Honesty, and Friendship Islands—they were like mini theme parks. The Emotions loved to watch the islands light up as they looked out the back window of Headquarters.

Riley had a very happy childhood, living with her parents in their small Minnesota town. She loved playing hockey, hanging out with her friends, and ice-skating on the lake. Joy made sure that at the end of each day, most of the memories rolling through Headquarters were golden, happy ones. But when Riley was eleven years old, her parents made a major decision that changed everything.

Riley's dad started a new business. Then her parents sold their home in Minnesota, and the family moved to San Francisco. Just like that, Riley's life was turned upside down.

The car ride across the country was long, and Riley's Emotions started to get restless. "Why don't we just live in this smelly car? We've already been in it forever," said Disgust, looking at the other Emotions.

Joy pointed out that the ride gave them plenty of time to imagine what the new house would look like. She plugged a cloud-shaped disc into the console as the Emotions reviewed all the great options they had thought up. Joy loved the image of the gingerbread house with the candy shutters. Anger liked the one of a dark castle that came with its very own fire-breathing dragon.

When Dad finally drove down their new block, the Emotions waited anxiously. They held their breath as Riley stepped out of the car and looked at the house . . .

It was NOTHING like what they had imagined.

"Maybe it's nice on the inside," Joy said cheerfully as she looked at the run-down Victorian.

But the inside was even worse! It was small, dark, and creepy, and it smelled weird. "We're supposed to live here?" Anger shouted.

"Do we have to?" Sadness said.

"Can you die from moving?" asked Fear nervously.

"I'm gonna be sick," said Disgust, noticing a dead mouse in the corner.

Joy reminded everyone how cool Dad said Riley's new bedroom was and suggested they check it out. Excited, Riley hurried upstairs to see it.

"No, no, no, no," said Fear, taking in the dismal view.

The room was ridiculously small, and it had a sloped ceiling, which made it feel even smaller. A gloomy mood fell over the Emotions.

"I'm starting to envy the dead mouse," said Disgust.

"Oh, Riley can't live here," added Sadness.

As usual, Joy tried to get everyone to look on the bright side. "I read somewhere that an empty room is an opportunity," she said excitedly. She got everybody to imagine how great the room would look with all of Riley's stuff set up. "We'll put the bed there. And the desk over there . . ." Soon, they were all thinking about how they could fix up the room.

"And the hockey lamp goes there . . . ," Fear added.

As they thought about Riley's posters, books, and glow-in-the-dark stars, they began to feel better. "Let's go get our stuff from the moving van!" Joy said.

Riley dashed back downstairs to see if the moving van had arrived yet. When she entered the living room, she saw Dad hang up the phone, and she could tell he was annoyed. "Well, guess what?" he said. "The moving van won't be here until Thursday!"

"You're kidding!" said Mom.

The news stressed out the family, and Mom and Dad began to argue. "You said it would be here yesterday!" said Mom.

"I know that's what I said," said Dad. "That's what they told me!"

The move to the new house was not off to a very good start.

Joy acted quickly. "I've got a great idea!" she said, clicking an idea bulb into the console.

Suddenly, Riley smiled. She grabbed her hockey stick and dropped a crumpled-up piece of paper on the floor. "Anderson makes her move. She's closing in!" Riley said playfully as she used her hockey stick to move the wad of paper across the floor like a puck.

"Oh, no you're not!" Dad said, grabbing a broom to use as a makeshift stick.

Riley slid across the hardwood floor in her socks as though she were on skates. She dribbled the paper toward the fireplace and whacked it in. "She shoots, and she scores! Woo-hoo!" Riley said, celebrating.

The Emotions cheered, and Joy turned to look out the back window of Headquarters. Family Island shone in the distance, powered up and running.

"Come on, Grandma!" Riley said as she skated around Mom.

"Grandma?" Mom said, putting her hair up in a ponytail. She grabbed a pillow to use as she played goalie, guarding the fireplace.

For a moment, the family forgot about their stress

and enjoyed playing together in the empty living room. A golden memory rolled through Headquarters.

Then Dad's phone rang, quickly ending the game.

"The investor's supposed to show up on Thursday, not today," he said after hanging up. "I gotta go."

"It's okay," said Mom. "We get it."

"You're the best," Dad said, and kissed Mom goodbye. "See you, sweetie," he said, waving at Riley.

"Dad just left us," said Fear.

"Oh, he doesn't love us anymore. That's sad," Sadness said, stepping up to the console. "I should drive, right?"

Joy quickly blocked her. "You know what I've realized?" she said, trying to come up with a way to turn the situation around. "Riley hasn't had lunch!" Joy yanked a memory sphere off the wall and played it, revealing a pizza shop Riley had noticed earlier, when they were in the car.

"Hey, I saw a pizza place down the street," Riley said to Mom. "Maybe we could try that?"

"Pizza sounds delicious," Mom said.

The Emotions cheered, and Joy smiled, happy to see that things were back on track.

3

"**W**HAT THE HECK IS THAT?!" shouted Fear as he watched Riley and her mother standing at the pizza counter, staring at a slice covered in broccoli.

"That's it. I'm done," said Disgust.

Anger fumed. "Congratulations, San Francisco, you've RUINED PIZZA! FIRST THE HAWAIIANS AND NOW YOU!" he shouted, shuddering as he thought about the pineapple that Hawaiians liked to add to their pizza.

As Riley and her mom walked home, the mood was somber. "What kind of a pizza place only serves one kind of pizza?" Mom asked.

Joy sighed as she glanced at the day's wall of multicolored memories and noticed there were not a whole lot of golden ones.

Then Riley and her mother started to talk about the long car trip to California. "What was your favorite part?" Mom asked Riley.

"Oh! What about the time with the dinosaur?" Joy said as she ran to the console to pull up the memory.

The happy memory was of Riley and her mom posing in front of a big cement dinosaur on the side of the road in Utah. As Dad knelt to get the shot, the car started to roll down the hill behind him! Riley and Mom tried to tell him, but he was too busy trying to take the perfect picture. By the time he finally noticed, it was too late. Dad ran after the car as it rolled in reverse and crashed into the tail of a cement stegosaurus!

"I liked that time at the dinosaur," Riley said, smiling. "That was pretty funny."

The Emotions chuckled as Riley enjoyed the memory. But then something strange happened. The memory turned BLUE and Riley's smile faded.

"Wait. What happened?" Joy asked as she spun around, trying to figure out what had gone wrong.

Her gaze landed on Sadness, who was standing right next to the memory.

"What did you do?" Joy asked.

"I just touched it," Sadness said.

Joy tried to rub the memory to see if she could change it back to gold, but the blue color wouldn't come off!

"Good going, Sadness," Disgust said. "Now when Riley thinks of that moment with Dad, she's gonna feel sad. Bravo."

"I'm—I'm sorry, Joy," Sadness stammered.

Joy told Sadness not to touch any memories until she figured out what was going on. Then she turned her attention back to Riley.

Riley and her mom were coming up to a set of stairs that led down a hill. The stairs had a railing. "Get ready! This is a monster railing, and we are riding it all the way down!" Joy said as she took control of the console.

Goofball Island, one of Riley's Islands of Personality, lit up with life as Riley sat on the banister, about to fly down. But then Riley changed her mind. She walked down the stairs instead.

"Wait, what? What happened?" Joy asked,

confused. She gasped as a memory rolled over her feet.

"A core memory!" cried Fear. Core memories powered Riley's Islands of Personality. If Riley's core memories weren't in the core memory holder, what was controlling her personality?

"Oh no," said Joy, picking up the memory. Everyone looked out the window to see a lifeless Goofball Island, completely dark and still.

Joy rushed to the core memory holder and saw Sadness standing right next to it! "Sadness!" she shouted. "What are you doing?"

"It looked like one was crooked, so I opened it and then it fell out! I . . . ," Sadness said, referring to a core memory. She had a hard time explaining herself.

Joy placed the memory back in the holder and everyone breathed a sigh of relief as Goofball Island started running again.

Riley ran up the stairs and jumped back on the railing. "Woo-hoo!" she cried as she slid down.

"I wanted to maybe hold one," Sadness admitted. She reached toward a core memory and it started to turn BLUE! As the other Emotions gasped, Joy grabbed Sadness's hand before she could remove it.

The memory turned back to gold.

"Sadness!" Joy scolded. "You nearly touched a core memory. And when you touch them, we can't change them back."

Sadness felt terrible. "I'm sorry," she said. "Something's wrong with me. I, uh . . . It's like I'm having a breakdown."

"You are not having a breakdown," said Joy. "It's stress."

Sadness sighed. "I keep making mistakes like that. I'm awful—"

"No, you're not," Joy interrupted, but Sadness continued.

"—and annoying."

Joy wanted Sadness to stop focusing on what was wrong. "There's always a way to turn things around, to find the fun," Joy said.

"I don't know how to do that," Sadness said.

Joy suggested that Sadness think of something funny, but she couldn't seem to do it. Sadness constantly focused on the negative. While Joy saw the rain as a fun opportunity for Riley to jump in puddles and carry a cool umbrella, Sadness liked when the rain made Riley feel soggy, droopy, and shivery. Sadness even started to cry as she thought about it.

"Oh, hey, hey . . . easy. Why are you crying?" Joy asked softly.

"Crying helps me slow down and obsess over the weight of life's problems," she said.

Joy put her head in her hands to think of a way to keep Sadness out of trouble. "Let's think about something else," she said, leading her over to the manual shelf. "How about we read some mind manuals, huh? Sounds fun."

Joy left Sadness among the stacks of books and marched back to work.

The first night in the new house was uncomfortable and creepy. Without furniture or a bed, Riley had to sleep in a sleeping bag on the floor. All the sounds of the city outside her window were loud and strange. Listening to the noises, Riley couldn't fall asleep.

Inside Headquarters, the Emotions were stressing out. "Was it a bear? It's a bear!" Fear said, controlling the console.

"There are no bears in San Francisco," Disgust said.

"I saw a really hairy guy," Anger said. "He *looked* like a bear."

"I'm so jumpy," Fear replied. "My nerves are shot!"

As Joy gazed at the memory shelves, the other Emotions talked about what a disaster the move had been. They blamed Joy for telling them that things wouldn't change when they moved. They had assumed they would be as happy in San Francisco as they had been in Minnesota.

Joy tried to reassure them. "Look, I get it. You guys have concerns, but we've been through worse!" But the other Emotions didn't see how the situation could possibly be any worse.

"Yeah, Joy. We could be lying on a dirty floor. In a sleeping bag," said Disgust sarcastically.

"But think of all the good things that—"

They didn't want to hear any more of Joy's positivity. "No, Joy," Anger interrupted. "There's absolutely no reason for Riley to be happy right now. Let us handle this."

"I say we skip school tomorrow and lock ourselves in the bedroom," Fear said.

"We have no clean clothes," Disgust agreed. "I mean, no one should see us."

"Yeah, we could cry until we can't breathe," Sadness offered.

Joy tried to get everyone to calm down. "Now hold

on," she said. "We all have our off days. You know, I . . ."

Then Mom appeared in Riley's doorway. "The Mom bad news train is pulling in," said Anger. "Toot, toot!"

Mom sat down next to Riley and gave her an update on the moving van: it was going to take even longer to arrive.

"Toot, toot, toot!" Anger shouted.

Joy sighed and backed away from the console as Mom went on to explain how stressed Dad was about his new business venture. Anger stepped up to the console, gearing up for some major scowling action.

But Mom surprised them. "I guess all I really want to say is thank you."

The Emotions were confused. Mom talked about how pleased she was that despite the rough situation, Riley had continued to be their happy girl. "Your dad's under a lot of pressure, but if you and I can keep smiling, it would be a big help. We can do that for him, right?" asked Mom.

Joy stepped up to the console proudly. She walked past Anger and took control. "Yeah, sure," Riley said, smiling.

"What did we do to deserve you?" Mom asked,

kissing Riley on the forehead. "Sweet dreams," she said as she walked out and closed the door.

All the Emotions smiled as they looked toward Joy. "Well," Anger said, "you can't argue with Mom. Happy it is."

"Team Happy! Sounds great," Fear said.

When Riley was finally asleep, the screen in Headquarters turned black. "Looks like we're going into REM," said Joy. Joy was on Dream Duty, which meant she had to stay up and monitor Riley's dreams. She'd also take care of sending the important memories to Long Term. "Great day today, guys. Sleep well, Team Happy!" Joy called to the other Emotions as they headed off to sleep.

Then she took her place at the console. "All right," she said, looking up at the screen. "What's on tonight, Dream Productions?" Joy couldn't wait to see what the movie studio in Riley's Mind World came up with for that evening.

The dream began with Riley's family happily flying through the sky in their car. Then the car landed in front of a frightening haunted house with a mouse ghost. The mouse looked like a zombie as it eerily said, "Come live with me, Riley." Then it keeled over and died!

"Who's in charge of programming down there?" Joy said, frowning. "I know I'm not supposed to do this, but . . ." She ducked behind the console and messed with a few wires and switches, resetting the system. "We are not going to end the day like this," she said.

Then she recalled a memory of Riley showcasing all of her ice-skating moves on the lake with her parents. Joy rigged it so the memory played in Riley's mind like a dream instead of what Dream Productions had put on. Joy skated around Headquarters, mimicking Riley and reliving the happy memory. She promised Riley that tomorrow would be another great day.

5

The next morning Joy was bursting with sunshine and positive energy. She played her accordion throughout Headquarters, trying to rouse the rest of the Emotions with a tune. "Hello! Did I wake you?" Joy yelled over the piercing sound of her instrument. The others were not so enthusiastic.

"Okay, first day of school!" Joy said, tossing her accordion aside. "Very exciting!" Riley was starting her new school today, and Joy had to make sure it went perfectly. Right away, she began getting everyone organized by assigning tasks. She asked Fear to come up with an extensive list of all the possible negative outcomes on the first day of school.

"Way ahead of you there," Fear said, scribbling in his notepad. "Does anyone know how to spell 'meteor'?"

"Disgust," Joy said. "Make sure Riley stands out today . . . but also blends in."

Disgust was on it. "When I'm through, Riley will look so good the other kids will look at their own outfits and barf," she said.

As Joy continued to prepare Headquarters, the Train of Thought chugged by and dropped off a bag. "Right on schedule," said Joy, smiling. "Anger, unload the daydreams. I ordered extra in case things get slow in class."

"Might come in handy if this new school is full of boring, useless classes, which it probably will be . . . ," Anger said as he walked toward the bag.

Sadness came out of the break room. "I have a super important job just for you," Joy said, approaching her.

"Really?" Sadness said.

Joy led Sadness to the back of the room and placed her in a special spot. "What are you doing?" Sadness asked.

Joy knelt down and used a piece of chalk to draw

a circle around Sadness's feet. "This is the circle of Sadness," Joy said. "Your job is to make sure that all the Sadness stays inside it."

Sadness was confused. "So . . . you want me to just stand here?"

"Hey, it's not MY place to tell you how to do your job," Joy said, nudging Sadness's foot so that it was inside the circle. "Just make sure that ALL the Sadness stays in the circle."

Joy knew that if the day was going to go well she had to keep Sadness as far from the controls as possible.

Sadness stood inside the circle, looking a little lost and confused. "You're a pro at this!" Joy cheered. "Isn't it fun?"

"No," Sadness said quietly as Joy walked back to the console.

"All right, everyone, fresh start!" Joy sang. "We are going to have a good day, which will turn into a good week, which will turn into a good year, which turns into a good LIFE!"

Riley was ready to go to school. She had her backpack on and was walking toward the front door.

"So, the big day!" Mom said, encouraging her with

a smile. "New school, new friends, huh?"

"I know! I'm kinda nervous, but I'm mostly excited! How do I look? Do you like my shirt?" Family Island was lighting up and working like crazy as Riley chatted away.

"You want us to walk with you?" Mom said.

Disgust quickly made the call on that one. "Mom and Dad? With us in public? No, thank you."

Joy took care of the situation by pressing a few buttons on the console.

"Nope! I'm fine," Riley said, upbeat. "Bye, Mom! Bye, Dad!"

"Have a good day at school, monkey," Dad said. Riley and her mom made monkey sounds as she walked out the door, which caused Goofball Island to power up.

Riley walked to her new school and stopped in front of the gate to take in the scene. There were tons of students, and the school was so big. "Are you sure we want to do this?" Fear said.

"In we go!" Joy said, totally ignoring Fear.

Riley smiled and walked up the steps to the school. Once she got inside, she found her classroom and sat down at a desk. The Emotions checked out the different groups of kids scattered around the room.

"Okay," said Disgust. "We've got a group of cool girls at two o'clock."

"How do you know?" asked Joy.

"Double ears pierced, infinity scarves . . ."

"Whoa," said Joy. "Is she wearing eye shadow?"

"Yeah, we want to be friends with them," said Disgust, who actually seemed excited.

Fear approached Joy. He was almost finished with his very long list of potential disasters. "Worst scenario is either quicksand, spontaneous combustion, or getting called on by the teacher," he said. "So as long as none of those happen . . ." His voice trailed off as the teacher addressed the class.

"Okay, everybody," she said, motioning for Riley to stand. "We have a new student in class today."

"Are you kidding me? Out of the gate? This is not happening!" Fear yelled.

Then the teacher asked Riley to introduce herself in front of everyone.

"Nooooooo!" Fear cried, flipping out. "Pretend we can't speak English!"

6

"**D**on't worry," said Joy. "I got this." She stepped in and pushed a lever on the console.

Riley smiled as she stood up and spoke to the class. "My name is Riley Anderson," she said. "I'm from Minnesota. And now I live here."

"And how about Minnesota?" the teacher asked. "Can you tell us something about it? Well, you certainly get a lot more snow than we do," she said.

Joy slapped her knee and laughed. "She's hilarious!" she said, turning a lever on the console.

Riley smiled as she told the class about Minnesota. She told them about the lake and how it froze over in the winter. She talked about being on an ice hockey team called the Prairie Dogs and playing with her friend Meg. Joy recalled a memory of the family skating together and played it on the screen.

Riley smiled, thinking about the memory, and continued to talk about playing hockey and how it was a family tradition. But then something very strange happened . . . the image on the screen that the Emotions were watching turned BLUE.

Riley's smile faded and her brow furrowed. Suddenly, she felt very sad. Joy and the other Emotions looked around confused until their eyes landed on Sadness, who was guiltily touching the memory sphere, which had also turned blue.

"Sadness!" Joy said, shocked. "You touched a memory!"

"Oh yeah, I know. I'm sorry," Sadness said.

"Get back in your circle," Joy snapped. Then she tried to eject the memory, but it wouldn't come out!

"Get it out of there, Joy!" Fear shouted.

"Cool kids whispering at three o'clock," Disgust said, pointing to the screen.

Inside the classroom, Riley was sniffling and some of the kids were whispering. "Did you see that look?"

Fear said, panicking. "They're judging us!"

Joy, Fear, Anger, and Disgust all tried to get the memory out, but it wouldn't budge. Riley's eyes welled up with tears as she continued. "But everything's different now," she said. "Since we moved . . ." Her voice trailed off and she was unable to speak.

"Oh no!" Fear shouted. "We're CRYING AT SCHOOL!"

Joy turned to the console to see SADNESS DRIVING! "What? No!" she shouted. Finally, she yanked the memory out and pulled Sadness off the controls. PING! A new memory had been created, and it was bright blue.

"Whoa!" Anger said.

"It's a core memory!" Fear shouted in awe.

"But it's blue!" Disgust said.

The bright blue memory rolled down the track as the core memory holder whirred into action. "No, wait!" Joy said, trying to stop it. She jumped and slapped her hand on the holder, popping the memory up and grabbing it. Then she leaned over and pressed the end-of-day Memory Dump button, causing the vacuum tube to come down from the ceiling. Joy got ready to send the blue core memory up, hoping it would be like it had never existed!

"Joy, no," Sadness said, running to save the memory. "That's a core memory!"

"Hey! Stop it," Joy said.

As the two struggled over the bright blue sphere, they bumped into the core memory holder and all the core memories fell out! Fear, Anger, and Disgust screamed as the Islands of Personality went DARK.

Joy quickly tossed the blue memory aside and scrambled as she tried to collect the core memories rolling around the floor like marbles. Sadness snatched up the blue core memory and moved to place it in the core memory holder, but Joy lunged and caused it to slip out of her hands. Then the powerful suction from the vacuum started to suck the blue core memory up through the tube!

Joy tumbled backward and dropped the memories she had gathered. Then the suction began to pull one of the gold core memories toward the tube. "No, no, no, no!" Joy shouted. She reached in to try to grab the memory and was sucked up with it! The intense suction pulled Sadness in, too!

Fear, Anger, and Disgust watched helplessly as Joy, Sadness, and the core memories were vacuumed up into the tube!

Back in the classroom, the teacher thanked Riley for sharing. Riley wiped her tears away as she sat down and awkwardly buried her head in her book.

Meanwhile, Joy and Sadness rocketed through the vacuum tube, clutching the core memories. Because they had never been out of Headquarters, they looked around in awe at parts of Riley's Mind World. As everything outside raced by, they couldn't help wondering: Where were they going to end up?

BLAM! Joy shot out of the tube and landed in a basket of memories. Sadness fell out next, crashing hard against the ground next to Joy. The core memories rolled in different directions. Joy frantically gathered them up. "One, two, three . . . okay. Where are we?"

Joy looked at the shelving units that surrounded them, and suddenly she realized they were in Long Term Memory. Grabbing the core memories, Joy hopped out of the memory basket. She could see Goofball Island in the distance, silent and dark. Beyond Goofball, the other islands were dark and lifeless, too.

Sadness walked up slowly behind Joy. "Riley's Islands of Personality. They're ALL down! Oh, this is bad, this is very, very bad," she whimpered.

"We—we can fix this," Joy stammered. "We just have to get back to Headquarters, plug the core memories in, and Riley will be back to normal."

With a sense of urgency, Joy and Sadness hurried toward Headquarters. "Riley has no core memories, no personality islands, and no . . ." Sadness stopped suddenly and gasped.

"What is it?" Joy asked.

"You!" Sadness declared. "YOU'RE not in Headquarters. Without you, Riley can't be happy."

Joy realized that Sadness was right. Together they crossed the bridge toward Goofball Island. She knew that if she could make it to the lightline, she could walk the power line that led from the core memory holder to the Islands of Personality, all the way back to Headquarters. "I'm coming, Riley," Joy said, determined. Headquarters loomed in the distance, the tallest structure in all of Mind World. It was going to be a long journey back.

That night, when Riley sat down to have dinner with her parents, she was quiet and distant.

Fear, Anger, and Disgust stood in Headquarters, stumped, as they looked at the empty core memory holder and the dark Islands of Personality.

"Riley is acting so weird," Disgust commented.

"What do you expect?" Anger demanded. "All the islands are down."

Disgust flipped her hair. "Joy would know what to do."

The three Emotions looked at one another as they came to a decision. They would do what Joy did until the missing Emotion returned. But there was a problem. None of them knew how to be happy.

"Hey, Riley," Mom said. "I've got good news! I found a junior hockey league right here in San Francisco. And get this: tryouts are tomorrow after school. What luck, right?"

"Pretend to be Joy," Fear said, quickly pushing a

reluctant Disgust toward the controls.

"Won't it be great to be back out on the ice?" Mom asked.

Disgust rolled her eyes as she pushed a few buttons.

"Oh yeah, that sounds fantastic," Riley replied sarcastically.

The look on Mom's face showed that she was clearly taken aback.

"What was that?" Fear asked. "That wasn't anything like Joy."

"Uh, because I'm NOT Joy," Disgust said.

Inside Mom's Headquarters, her Emotions were scrambling to assess the situation. "Did you guys pick up on that?" Mom's Sadness asked. Her other Emotions nodded. "Let's probe," Mom's Sadness said. "But keep it subtle so she doesn't notice."

"So, how was the first day of school?" Mom asked.

"She's probing us," Anger said.

"I'm done," said Disgust. She turned to Fear. "YOU pretend to be Joy."

"What? Uh . . . okay," Fear said, awkwardly stepping up to the controls.

But Fear wasn't any better at helping Riley act like herself than Disgust. Riley continued to sound strange, and her mom noticed.

Inside Mom's Headquarters, her Emotions decided to take a different approach. "Signal the husband," Mom's Sadness said.

Mom tried to signal Dad, but inside his Headquarters, his Emotions were busy watching a hockey match. Finally, Mom's signal worked. "Uh-oh," Dad's Anger said. "She's looking at us." He clicked off the hockey game and tried to pay attention.

Mom raised her eyebrows at him, signaling him again as he stared at her blankly, wondering what she was trying to say. Finally, he got it. "Ahhh, so, Riley! How was school?" he asked.

Inside Riley's Headquarters, Anger had had enough. "Move," he said, marching up to the console. "I'LL be Joy."

"School was great, all right?" Riley's voice was full of attitude.

"Riley, is everything okay?" Mom asked, concerned.

Riley rolled her eyes and let out a dramatic groan.

Inside Dad's Headquarters, his Emotions finally noticed Riley's odd behavior. "Sir, she just rolled her eyes at us," Dad's Fear said.

"Riley, I do NOT like this new attitude," Dad said.

"Oh, I'll show you attitude, old man," Anger said, steaming up.

"No!" Fear said, trying to stop Anger from exploding. "Stay happy!" But Anger shoved him away and forcefully hit a button on the console.

"What is your problem? Just leave me alone," said Riley.

Like a soldier, Dad's Fear reported "high levels of sass," and his Emotions took it to DEFCON 2, the highest level of alert before things got really bad. The siren inside Dad's Headquarters blared and his Emotions prepared to "put the foot down."

Inside Riley's mind, Anger had really worked himself up. "You want a piece of this, Pops? Come and get it!" he yelled, and with all his might, he pushed two levers as far forward as they would go.

"Just shut up!" Riley yelled.

"Fire!" yelled Dad's Anger, like a sergeant.

"That's it!" Dad yelled. "Go to your room! Now!"

Riley pushed her chair away from the table and stomped upstairs to her bedroom.

"The foot is down! The foot is down!" Dad's Fear announced. All the Emotions inside Dad's mind cheered.

"Good job, gentlemen," Dad's Anger said. "That could have been a disaster."

Mom's Emotions sighed with disappointment. "Well, that was a disaster," Mom's Sadness said.

Once Riley got to her bedroom, she slammed the door behind her.

8

Joy and Sadness had finally made it across the bridge to Goofball Island and stepped carefully onto the lightline. Joy looked down into the deep darkness of the Memory Dump that loomed below her.

Sadness was afraid, but walking the tightrope of the lightline was the quickest way back. "If we fall," she protested, pointing down at the Memory Dump, "we'll be forgotten forever."

"We have to do this," Joy said, trying to reassure her. "For Riley. Just follow my footsteps."

Holding the memories in her arms, Joy tried to balance herself on the narrow line. One of the memories slipped over the side, but she snatched it back just in time. She breathed and slowly began the long, treacherous trip toward Headquarters with Sadness right behind her. Joy wished she knew what was happening with Riley.

Tap, tap, tap. Dad knocked on Riley's bedroom door and peeked inside. "Hey," he said.

Riley lay in her sleeping bag on the floor, silent and motionless. "So, uh . . . ," Dad said gently. "Things got a little out of hand downstairs." He waited for Riley to respond, but she remained silent.

"You want to talk about it? Come on, where's my happy girl? Monkey," Dad said. "Oo oo ooo!" He made silly monkey sounds, trying to cheer her up.

The Emotions could see he was trying to start up Goofball Island. Fear looked at the empty core memory holder and then out the window at Goofball Island. It was still dark.

Riley didn't respond or laugh like she normally would when her dad acted silly. Instead, she glanced at him before rolling over to face the wall.

Rrrrrrrrrck. Goofball Island made an awful groaning noise and shuddered like an old, tired ship. Suddenly, bits and pieces of the island began to crumble away!

Joy and Sadness, who were still balancing on the lightline connected to the island, felt it tremble beneath their feet as Goofball Island started to disintegrate. The lightline was falling! They had to get off it now! "Run! Run! Run!" Joy screamed.

Frantically they dashed back to Goofball Island, barely outracing the crumbling pieces of land.

At the edge of the island, the bridge twisted and buckled underneath them. They managed to stay on their feet as they reached one of the cliffs of Long Term Memory just as the memory tube and basket they had arrived in broke off and fell into the Memory Dump below.

From the safety of solid ground, they watched in horror as Goofball Island sank and vanished into the dump. The island was GONE. Joy gasped. "What . . . ?"

Inside Riley's bedroom, Dad was telling her that he understood and that he thought she probably needed some alone time. "We'll talk later," he said as he left the room.

Fear, Anger, and Disgust stared out the back window of Headquarters, stunned.

"We have a major problem," said Disgust.

"Oh, Joy, where are you?" whined Fear.

9

Joy and Sadness gazed down over the edge of the cliff at the endless drop below. They couldn't believe it: a huge hollow space hung where Goofball Island used to be. The island had completely disappeared.

Sadness was immediately worried. "We lost Goofball Island. That means she can lose Friendship and Hockey and Honesty and Family," she said. She turned to Joy. "You can fix this, right?"

"I . . . I don't know," admitted Joy, feeling lost.

Sadness's groan of despair was enough to kick-start Joy's optimism. "But we have to try. Okay? Come on."

Joy's eyes fell on Friendship Island as the sky

began to darken. "Riley's gone to sleep, which is a good thing. Nothing else bad can happen while she's asleep and we'll be back to Headquarters before she wakes up," Joy said. "We'll just go across Friendship Island."

When Sadness noticed there was no way to get there along the edge of the cliff, she moaned. "We'll never make it, hoh . . . no . . ."

Joy reached for Sadness, knowing she was on the edge of collapse. "No, no, no, don't obsess over the weight of life's problems. Remember that funny movie where the dog dies?"

Sadness thought for a minute. Finally, she slumped down to the ground in a face-plant of despair.

"Sadness, we don't have time for this," Joy said.

Joy looked around, trying to figure out the best way back to Headquarters. She saw stacks of memory shelves winding off into the distance. "We'll have to go around. Take the scenic route," she said. She took a deep breath and set off.

"Wait! Joy, you could get lost in there!" Sadness shouted after her.

"Think positive!" Joy reminded her.

"Okay," Sadness said. "I'm positive you will get

lost in there! That's Long Term Memory. I read about it in the manual."

Joy's eyes popped wide open. "The manual?" she cried. "The manual! You read the manual!"

Sadness had had lots of time to read about Long Term Memory while she was sitting in the "Circle of Sadness."

Joy ran back to Sadness. "So you know the way back to Headquarters?"

Sadness was confused. "I guess . . ."

"Congratulations," Joy beamed. "You are the official Mind Map."

Sadness didn't know how to respond. "Thank you?"

"Let's go! Lead on, Mind Map. Show me where we're going."

Sadness nodded, but she didn't move. "Okay! Only . . . I'm too sad to walk. Just give me a few hours."

Joy was not about to let Sadness's emotional slump slow them down. Determined, she picked up one of Sadness's legs and dragged her into the labyrinth. "Which way?" Joy asked. "Left?"

"Right," Sadness said. Joy turned right. "No, I mean, go left. I said left was right. Like 'correct.'"

"Okay," Joy said, moving on.

"This actually feels kinda nice," Sadness said as Joy picked up the pace, pulling her through the maze.

"This is working!" Joy said.

Out of breath and sweating, Joy continued to drag Sadness. They were lost. "This is not working. Are we getting close?"

"Just another right . . . and a left. Then another left, and a right . . . ," Sadness said.

Joy simply grunted in frustration and kept moving.

10

When the sky finally brightened, Joy was *still* dragging Sadness through the winding memory shelves. "Riley's awake," Joy said with a sigh. She couldn't believe they had walked the entire night and they were still trying to get through Long Term Memory. She wondered if they were any closer to getting out than they had been when they started.

Joy dropped the core memories and Sadness reached out to touch them. "Ah ah ah, don't touch, remember? If you touch them, they stay sad," Joy reminded her.

"Sorry," said Sadness. "I won't."

Joy looked back to see all the bottom rows of the memories on the shelves they had passed: they were now *all blue*.

"Starting now," Sadness added.

Joy dropped her head in her hands. "Ugh," she groaned. "I can't take much more of this."

But then she brightened as she heard voices among the shelves. "Mind workers!" she said, racing off in search of the voices.

"But, Joy, we're almost . . . ," Sadness called after her. "Ohhh."

Joy slipped down an aisle and found two pear-shaped mind workers wearing helmets and goggles. They were vacuuming memories off the shelves. One held a clipboard while the other sucked up memories with the vacuum. "Look at this," said the first worker, pointing out some memory spheres. "Four years of piano lessons."

"Yeah, looks pretty faded," said the other worker, assessing them.

"You know what?" the first worker said. "Save 'Chopsticks' and 'Heart and Soul' and get rid of the rest."

ZOOP! The worker used the vacuum to suck up

the memories. Joy was shocked. She asked them why they were vacuuming up perfectly good memories.

The workers introduced themselves—they were Forgetters. They explained that their job was to clear out Riley's faded memories and send them to the Memory Dump.

"Nothing comes back from the dump," the Forgetter holding the clipboard said. "When Riley doesn't care about a memory, it fades."

"Fades?" Joy asked, confused. This was the first time she had heard about memories fading.

"Happens to the best of 'em," the Forgetter said.

"Except for this bad boy!" the other Forgetter said with a chuckle. "This one will *never* fade." Grinning, he pulled out a memory from a nearby shelf and showed it to Joy.

"The song from the gum commercial?" Joy asked. The memory was of a Tripledent gum commercial that had a catchy tune.

The Forgetters laughed as they played the memory again. "You know, sometimes we send that up to Headquarters for no reason," the first Forgetter said.

"It just plays in Riley's head over and over again," the other Forgetter added. "Like a million times!"

They laughed as they watched the commercial again, and cracked up even more as they sang along.

Joy watched as the worker put the memory on the shelf and pushed it toward the back. FWOOM! It shot through a tube out of the top of a shelf and up toward Headquarters.

Meanwhile, Riley was in her bedroom on her laptop, talking to her best friend Meg from Minnesota.

"Do you like it there?" Meg asked. "Did you feel any earthquakes? Is the bridge cool?"

"Yeah," Riley replied somberly. "It's good. . . . What happened with the playoffs?"

Meg went on to tell Riley that the Prairie Dogs had won their first game. She told her about a new girl on the team. "She's so cool," Meg said.

"Oh, she did *not* just say that," Disgust said, her voice dripping with attitude.

"A *new girl*?" Fear said, panicking. "Meg has a new friend already?!"

"GRRRRRRRRRR!" Anger growled.

"Hey, hey, stay happy!" Disgust coached. "We do NOT want to lose any more islands here, guys."

But Meg continued to tell Riley how she and the new girl passed the puck to each other without even looking. "It's like mind reading!" Meg said.

Anger grabbed the controls. "You like to read minds, Meg?" he shouted. "I got something for you to read right here!"

"Hey, no, no, no, what are you doing?" Disgust asked.

"Let's just be calm for one second," Fear advised as Anger pulled Fear's nose out and let it snap back like a rubber band.

With no one holding him back, Anger pushed the gear full steam ahead.

"I gotta go," Riley said, cutting Meg off. Then she slammed down the lid of her laptop and hung up on her.

Joy, still listening to the Forgetters laugh about their gum commercial prank, heard a horrible *crrrreak* from outside the memory shelves. She ran to see what it was.

"Oh no," she cried, taking in the sight. Friendship Island was falling apart!

Joy looked down at the Friendship core memory in her arms; it was fading. Inside the memory sphere she could see the faint image of little Riley and Meg, skipping over cracks in the sidewalk, laughing and having fun.

Joy watched as the broken island completely sank into the darkness below. "Ohhh, not Friendship," she said.

Sadness walked up to her, having witnessed the whole thing. "Oh, Riley loved that one," she said. "And now it's *gone*." Sadness couldn't help herself, and she continued. "Goodbye, Friendship. Hello, loneliness."

Joy's expression fell. Then she scanned the area. She eyed Hockey Island in the hazy distance and set her sights on a solution. "We'll just have to go the long way," she said.

"Yeah," said Sadness. "The long . . . long . . . long way. I'm ready." She collapsed onto the ground and kicked her leg up, offering it to Joy.

Joy sighed as she once again started to pull Sadness by the leg through the winding memory shelves. "There's gotta be a better way," she said.

She heard someone humming, and in the distance she could see a large pink elephant happily grabbing memories from the shelves.

11

"**O**h, look at you," the elephant figure cried as he grabbed one particular memory. "You're a keeper!"

Joy continued to watch him from a distance.

The figure was so intent on picking memories that he didn't see Joy until she stepped forward. "Hello!"

When the elephant locked eyes with Joy, he froze—and then ran. He tried to get away, but Joy chased him until he reached a wall and began frantically to try to climb it. He was a strange-looking pink creature with a long trunk, whiskers, and a fluffy striped tail. He wore a checkered coat that was too small for his body and had a tiny hat perched on top of his head.

"Excuse me," Joy said, trying not to scare him more than he already was.

The creature jumped, startled, and screamed. "Ahh!" Feeling cornered, he grabbed a random memory off the wall and threw it at Joy. "Ha ha, so long, sucker!" But he ran right into a cart of memories and fell to the ground, taking the memories with him.

"Wait," said Joy, recognizing his face. "I know you."

"I get that a lot," he said nervously. "I look like a lot of people."

Joy gasped, finally placing his face. "You're Bing Bong, Riley's imaginary friend!"

"You *do* know me!" Bing Bong said, pleasantly surprised.

"Riley loved playing with you!" Joy exclaimed. "Oh, you would know. We're trying to get back to Headquarters. . . ."

"You guys are from Headquarters?" Bing Bong asked.

"Well, yeah. I'm Joy. This is Sadness."

"You're Joy? *The* Joy?" Bing Bong gasped. "Without you, Riley won't ever be happy. And we can't have that. We gotta get you back. I'll tell you what, follow me!"

Joy thanked Bing Bong for his help as the three of them walked down a long corridor of memory shelves. "It is so great to see you again," Joy said.

She remembered how Riley and Bing Bong had held concerts with pots and pans as their instruments; how they had raced each other, with Bing Bong on the ceiling and Riley on the floor; and how Bing Bong's red rocket ship wagon ran on song power.

Joy even remembered the theme song Riley made up that powered the rocket ship. Bing Bong and Joy sang the happy tune together as Sadness finally took a good look at him. "What exactly are you supposed to be?" she asked.

"You know, it's unclear," Bing Bong said. "I'm mostly cotton candy, but shape-wise, I'm part cat, part elephant, and part dolphin."

"Dolphin?" Joy asked. She didn't really see much evidence of a dolphin in Bing Bong.

Then he let out a high-pitched noise that sounded just like a dophin!

Joy asked Bing Bong what he was doing in the memory shelves. Bing Bong explained that there wasn't much need for an imaginary friend in Riley's life lately. He thought maybe if he could find a really good memory, Riley would remember him and he could be part of her life again.

"Hey, hey, don't be sad," Joy told him. "When I get back to Headquarters, I'll make sure Riley remembers you."

Bing Bong was thrilled. He began to dance around in excitement, but ended up tripping over his own feet. "Dooooh!" he cried.

Joy and Sadness watched as pieces of candy fell out of his eyes. "What's going on?" Sadness asked.

"I cry candy," Bing Bong said, in tears. "Try the caramel, it's delicious."

Joy munched on one of his sweet candy tears as she shifted the core memories around in her arms. The spheres were heavy and slippery, and it was a challenge keeping them all together.

"Oh—here, use this," Bing Bong said, dumping the contents of his little bag onto the floor. Joy and Sadness watched with amazement as an insanely large pile of random stuff fell out—memories, three boots, a hissing cat, and even a kitchen sink! "What?" Bing Bong shrugged. "It's imaginary."

"This'll make it a lot easier to walk back to Headquarters," Joy said with relief, putting the core memories safely into the bag.

"We're not walking. We're taking the Train of Thought!" Bing Bong led them out onto a cliff edge and pointed at the train speedily chugging toward Headquarters in the distance.

"The train, of course!" Joy exclaimed. "That is so much faster!"

Bing Bong told them about a station in Imagination Land, another part of Riley's Memory World, where they could catch the train. He said he could take them there. "I know a shortcut," he said proudly. "Come on, this way!"

"I'm so glad we ran into you," said Joy.

Bing Bong led the way to a huge bunker-like building. They looked through a window and straight out another window on the opposite side of the building. There was the train station.

Bing Bong opened a large, sturdy hatch door. "After you."

Joy took her first step into the building but stopped when Sadness called her.

"I read about this place in the manual. We shouldn't go in there," Sadness said.

"Bing Bong says it's the quickest way to Headquarters."

"But, Joy, this is Abstract Thought," Sadness explained.

"What're you talking about?" asked Bing Bong. "I go in here all the time. It's a shortcut, you see?" Bing Bong pointed to a sign hanging above the door and spelled it aloud: "'D-A-N-G-E-R.' That spells 'SHORTCUT.' I'll prove it to you." Joy and Sadness watched as Bing Bong climbed through the hatch.

12

"Look at me! I'm closer to the station 'cause I'm taking the shortcut!" Bing Bong sang from inside.

"Let's go around. This way." Sadness pointed to the path alongside the incredibly long building. Joy looked back at Bing Bong.

"Almost there!" Bing Bong shouted.

Joy turned to Sadness. "If you want to walk the long way, go for it. But Riley needs to be happy. I'm not missing that train," Joy said. "Bing Bong knows what he's doing. He's part dolphin. They're very smart!" she added.

"Well . . . I guess . . . ," Sadness said, following Joy

through the hatch and into the building.

Inside, it was dark and gray. There were strange shapes scattered all around.

Outside, two mind workers wheeled a cart over to the hatch they had just entered. They didn't realize that Bing Bong, Sadness, and Joy were inside the building.

"Okay, what Abstract Concept are we trying to comprehend today?" one worker asked.

"Um . . . loneliness," said the other worker, checking his clipboard.

"Looks like there's something in there," said the first worker, peering into the hatch. "I'm going to turn it on for a minute and burn out the gunk." The worker closed the door and Joy, Sadness, and Bing Bong heard a slam.

Suddenly, the room brightened as white lights flickered on. Strange shapes floated up off the floor and hung in the air.

"Say, would you look at that," said Bing Bong, marveling at the sight.

One of the shapes swiped by underneath Joy's feet. "Whoa!" she yelled.

Sadness ducked out of the way as another shape

On the day Riley was born, a new world was created:
Riley's Mind World.

Joy lived in Headquarters inside Riley's Mind World.
There she saw everything through Riley's eyes.

When Riley's parents looked down at her for the first time,
Joy watched in amazement.

A glowing sphere rolled into Headquarters.
When Joy picked it up, she realized it was the memory
of what she had just witnessed.

Riley started to cry, and a new Emotion appeared next to
Joy at the console. Her name was Sadness.

Before long, more Emotions arrived in Headquarters.
Fear kept Riley safe. Disgust kept close watch for anything
that required an "Ew."

Anger helped Riley deal with all the injustices of life. When he was in charge of the console, it was best to stay out of the way.

The Emotions looked out the back window of Headquarters at Riley's Islands of Personality. The islands made Riley who she was. They each represented an important part of her personality.

Riley was a happy girl, which meant that Joy was usually the one in charge of the console.

When Riley was eleven, her family moved from Minnesota to San Francisco. The change was a little scary, but also exciting— and they got to eat a lot of takeout!

On the first day at her new school, Riley got sad when she started talking about her old life in Minnesota.

Joy quickly played a happy memory, but Riley started to cry when Sadness touched it.

Inside Dream Productions, Joy, Sadness, and Riley's imaginary friend, Bing Bong, came up with a plan to get back to Headquarters and save Riley.

Things didn't go according to plan, but at least Bing Bong, Joy, and Sadness were able to continue on their way back to Headquarters.

Joy, Sadness, and Bing Bong rode on
the Train of Thought.

Back in Headquarters, Joy and Sadness realized that by working
together, they could help Riley become happy again.

whizzed closely by her head. "Ah!"

"What's happening?" Joy cried.

"Oh no," said Sadness. "They turned it on."

"Huh! I've never seen this before," said Bing Bong, watching as the floating shapes started to melt.

Joy and Sadness screamed as they took in the sight of Bing Bong's head: it had transformed into a misshapen mess and made him look like a multifaceted figure from a Picasso painting. His trunk looked like a jagged staircase, and one of his eyes moved over to the now-flat side of his head!

Then the same thing happened to Joy and Sadness! Their bodies shuffled around, as if they were built out of tiny cubes that made them look like weird, mixed-up versions of their former selves. All their body parts were twisted around and in the wrong places!

"What is going on?" Joy cried, feeling her nose shift up to the top of her head.

"We're abstracting!" screamed Sadness. Her mouth moved to where her right ear used to be, and her eyes were stacked on top of each other! "There are four stages. This is the first: nonobjective fragmentation!"

They struggled to walk, their bodies moving stiffly without knees and elbows.

"All right, don't panic!" said Bing Bong. "What's important is that we all *stay together*."

Suddenly, Bing Bong's left arm fell off! Joy screamed as her head fell off! Then Sadness's right leg fell off, causing her to topple over.

"We're in the second stage," Sadness said. "We're deconstructing!"

All three of them separated into pieces, like dolls that had been taken apart. "Ahh!" screamed Bing Bong. "I can't feel my legs!" Bing Bong's arms found his legs and grabbed them. "Oh, there they are."

Joy tried to put herself back together again and grabbed Sadness's leg instead. She slapped it on and looked like a mismatched puzzle.

Sadness chased after her disassembled head. "We've got to get out of here before we're nothing but shape and color and get stuck here forever!" she screamed.

"Stuck? Why did we come in here?" Joy yelled.

"I told you, it's a shortcut!" said Bing Bong.

They could hear the train whistling outside and watched through the window as it pulled into the station. "The train!" Joy cried.

POP! Joy, Sadness, and Bing Bong changed form

once again. Now they were flat!

"Oh no," said Sadness. "We're two-dimensional! That's stage three!"

"Depth!" yelped Bing Bong. "I'm lacking depth!"

They struggled to make their way through the strange, flat world. Things that seemed close by took a long time to reach. Doors that seemed just their size suddenly became too small when they tried to walk through them. "We can't fit!" grunted Joy, trying to squeeze through.

POP! They changed again. Now they were shapeless blobs of color, like lumps of clay.

"Oh no, we're nonfigurative," said Sadness. "This is the last stage!"

"We're not going to make it!" said Bing Bong.

Sadness hit the ground and instantly transformed into a blue line. "Wait!" she said. "We're two-dimensional. Fall on your face!" She crawled like an inchworm along the ground.

Joy and Bing Bong followed Sadness's lead and fell, turning into lines of color, too. They wiggled and squirmed right through the window!

TOOT, TOOT! The train whistled as it prepared to leave the station.

"Wait! Stop!" Joy yelled. She tried to jump but couldn't.

POP! Joy changed back into her two-dimensional shape and fell down flat. She looked up at the passing train. "Nooooo!" she said, defeated, watching as the train chugged and puffed its way toward Headquarters.

She turned to Bing Bong. "How long until the next train?"

He shrugged. "Who knows?"

"But don't worry. There's another station," said Bing Bong in a comforting voice as they all popped back into their original three-dimensional selves. "If we hurry, we can catch it."

Joy was skeptical, wondering if they were simply headed on another of Bing Bong's shortcuts. As he walked ahead, she whispered to Sadness, "Is there really another station?"

"Uh-huh," Sadness said. "Through there."

Straight ahead, Bing Bong stood with his arms held wide in front of big, beautiful gates. "Welcome to Imagination Land," he declared.

"Imagination Land?" Joy asked.

"Sure, I come here all the time. I'm practically the mayor. Hey, you guys hungry?" he asked. "There's French Fry Forest!"

"No way." Joy's eyes grew wide as she looked at the small area filled with giant French fries.

The next area Bing Bong led them to was full of glittering trophies and medals. "Check it out. Trophy Town! Medals, ribbons, certificates . . . everyone's a winner," he said, before kicking a soccer ball into a goal. Mind workers immediately rushed to him and showered him with medals. "I won first place!" he shouted.

Down the way, Joy spotted Cloud Town and got even more excited. "That's my favorite!" she said, ripping off a small chunk of cloud. She held on as the little piece of cloud floated her up into the air. She quickly let go and ran off to see more of Imagination Land.

Bing Bong stared at the cloud. Then he ripped off a piece, too. But it wasn't just a random cloud in Cloud Town—it was part of a cloud house. A cloud man stomped angrily from the front door. Startled, Bing Bong took a deep breath and blew out, pushing the cloud man away.

Swiftly, the three moved on to the land of Lava! There, Joy and Bing Bong jumped on big couches, moving from cushion to cushion over the lava and having a great time. "Imagination Land is the best!" shouted Bing Bong.

Sadness didn't agree. "Is it all going to be so interactive?" she asked.

"Wait, wait! Hang on just a minute," Bing Bong said as he spied a house made of giant playing cards.

Joy and Sadness watched as he rushed into the house and emerged with a red rocket ship wagon. Joy was so excited to see it. "I stashed it in there for safekeeping," Bing Bong explained. "Now I'm all set to take Riley to the moon!"

Bing Bong flung his arms wide and accidentally hit the card house. One by one, the cards collapsed on one another until the house disappeared. Joy, Sadness, and Bing Bong moved on to another area.

"Isn't it great?" asked Bing Bong as he looked around Imagination Land. "And there's always something new, like . . . Who the heck is that?" Bing Bong stopped and pointed to a handsome teenage boy leaning against a wall, striking a pose.

A worker passing by answered, "Imaginary Boyfriend."

"I would die for Riley," said Imaginary Boyfriend in a dramatic, raspy voice.

"Oh, gaah," said Joy, her lip curling in disgust.

"I've never seen him before," said Bing Bong.

"I live in Canada," the boyfriend said quickly.

Joy was anxious to get to the train. "This way, through Preschool World," Bing Bong said as he guided them.

"Riley, here we come!" Joy exclaimed.

Meanwhile, Riley was inside a local hockey rink. She was sitting on the bleachers next to her mom, getting ready for tryouts. "These kids look pretty good considering they're from San Francisco," her mom said jokingly.

"Okay, Anderson, you're up!" the coach shouted.

"I gotta go," said Riley as she stood. Then she skated onto the ice.

Inside Headquarters, Disgust, Fear, and Anger were racking their brains, trying to figure out what to do. With the core memories gone, the Islands of Personality were all dark. That meant that when Riley went to use one, she wouldn't be able to. "If she tries to use Hockey Island, it's going down," said Disgust.

"Which is why I've recalled every hockey memory I can think of," said Fear. "One of these has got to work in place of the core memory."

They started loading the memories into the core memory holder as Riley skated onto the ice. Out the back window, the Emotions could see Hockey Island sputtering, lighting up weakly. "Ha ha!" Fear cried. "We did it! It's working!"

BOOM! Suddenly, the holder blew out one of the memories like a bullet and took Anger right along with it! "Umph!" Anger groaned as the memory knocked into him.

On the ice, Riley struggled to control the puck. She went to slap it but missed and fell flat on her back.

Inside Headquarters, Fear tried to jam the memory back into the holder, but it shot out again and blew him back. Then the holder spun like a top and blasted all the memories out, spitting them at Fear! He collapsed to the ground, in pain.

Riley continued to fumble on the ice. She looked

like she had never played hockey before. She tried to slap the puck and fell down again.

"That's it!" Anger said, pushing Fear off the controls.

"Wait," Fear said. "No, no, no! Use your words."

"GrrraaaAAHHH!" Anger screamed.

Riley snapped. She threw down her hockey stick. The other players stopped in their tracks to watch as she rushed off the ice, back to the bleachers.

"Riley, what's wrong?" Mom asked.

"Let's go," Riley said, taking off her skates.

"You're not going to finish tryouts?"

"What's the point?"

"Hey, it'll be all right," Mom said. "Let's just—"

Riley exploded. "Stop saying everything will be all right!" she yelled. Then she dashed toward the exit.

Back in Imagination Land, Joy heard a deafening BOOM! She turned to watch Hockey Island crumble like an iceberg. Another island was gone.

14

"**B**ing Bong, we have to get to that station," Joy said. She couldn't believe they had lost another island. The train whistled in the distance, which made her feel even more anxious.

"Sure thing," Bing Bong said. "This way, just past Graham Cracker Castle." But then he stopped and looked around, confused. The castle was gone. "I wonder why they moved it?" he asked. He walked a bit farther. Suddenly, he realized things didn't look right.

A giant bulldozer came hurtling toward him and knocked over a pink castle. Bing Bong gasped.

"Princess Dream World!" Glitter flew into the air as the castle disintegrated. All of Preschool World was being torn down!

"My rocket!" Bing Bong screamed as he saw the Forgetters walking by with a red wagon. He ran after it. "Wait!" he yelled as a bulldozer pushed the pile of old memories closer and closer to the cliff edge. "Riley and I were still using that rocket! It still has some song power left!"

He desperately sang the song that powered the rocket and it responded, *bing*ing and *bong*ing back at him and firing up. It rocketed into the air, then dove straight over the cliff! "Nooo!" Bing Bong screamed. "You can't take my rocket to the dump! Riley and I are going to the *moon*!" He watched in shock as the rocket disappeared into the infinite darkness of the dump below. "Riley *can't* be done with me," he said, feeling heartbroken and falling to his knees.

Joy could think of only one thing: she had to get to the station. So she tried to pep Bing Bong up. "Hey, it's going to be okay. We can fix this. We just need to get back to Headquarters. Which way to the train station?" Bing Bong had no reaction. He was frozen with grief.

"I had a whole trip planned for us," he said quietly.

"Here comes the tickle monster," Joy said, as she tried a different tactic. She tickled him, but he didn't respond. She even tried making funny faces, but her silliness wasn't snapping Bing Bong out of his misery. "Oh, here comes a fun game. You point to the train station, and we'll go there," Joy said. Bing Bong remained motionless.

Sadness walked over and sat down next to him. "I'm sorry they took your rocket," she said gently. "They took something that you loved and it's gone . . . forever."

"Sadness, don't make him feel worse," Joy said.

"Sorry," said Sadness.

"It's all I had left of Riley," said Bing Bong.

"I bet you and Riley had great adventures," Sadness said.

"They were wonderful. Once, we flew back in time. We had breakfast twice that day."

"That sounds amazing. I bet Riley liked it."

"Oh, she did. We were best friends," Bing Bong said. He started to cry.

"Yeah," said Sadness. "It is sad."

Bing Bong put his head on Sadness's shoulder and cried candy tears. Sadness put her arm around him and tried to comfort him as he sobbed.

After a good cry, Bing Bong wiped his eyes and took a deep breath. "I'm okay now," he said with a sniffle. He stood up and looked around. "C'mon. The train station is this way." He started to walk toward it.

Joy looked at Sadness in disbelief. "How did you do that?" she asked.

"I don't know," said Sadness. "He was sad, so I listened to what—"

"Hey, there's the train!" Bing Bong called.

The three ran up to the train and climbed aboard just as it was starting up. "We made it!" Joy said. "We're finally going to get home!"

Back in Headquarters, Anger, Fear, and Disgust ranted about the terrible day they'd had. "On a scale of one to ten, I give this day an F," said Disgust.

"Well, why don't we quit standing around and do something," Anger suggested, dropping his newspaper, which was emblazoned with the headline "Riley Quits Hockey!"

Fear thought they all should quit their jobs as Riley's Emotions. He knew it was the coward's way out, but since he was Fear, he was okay with that.

"Emotions don't quit, genius," Disgust said.

Suddenly, Anger ran to the back and rummaged through the ideas, looking for something. "Aha!" he shouted, holding up an idea bulb triumphantly. He believed he'd found the solution they needed to fix everything for Riley. "Just the best idea ever!" he announced.

"What?" Disgust asked.

"All the good core memories were made in Minnesota," Anger said. "Ergo, we go back to Minnesota and make more. Ta-da!"

"Wait, wait, wait. You're saying we run away?" asked Fear. "You can't be serious."

"Our life was perfect until Mom and Dad decided to move to San Fran Stinktown," said Anger.

"But, I mean, it's just so . . . drastic," said Fear.

"Need I remind you how great things were there? Our room? Our backyard? Our *friends*?" Anger punched up a memory, playing it on the screen.

The Tripledent gum commercial song played throughout Headquarters. "Did I ask for the gum commercial?" Annoyed, Anger slapped his hand against the console, ejecting the memory. "Anyway, it was better. That's my point."

"Yeah, Riley was happier in Minnesota . . . ," said

Disgust, nodding her head.

"Shouldn't we just sleep on it or something?" asked Fear.

"Fine. Let's sleep on it," Anger said, crossing his arms over his chest. "Because hey—I'm sure jolly, fun-filled times are just around the corner."

Inside her bedroom, Riley drifted off to sleep.

With Riley asleep, day turned to night in Mind World and the Train of Thought came to a screeching halt. "Huh?" Joy was confused. "Hey! Why aren't we moving?"

"Riley's gone to sleep," the train engineer said. "We're all on break."

"You mean we're stuck here until morning?" asked Sadness.

"Yeah, the Train of Thought doesn't run while she's asleep," answered Bing Bong.

"Oh, we can't wait that long!" groaned Joy.

15

Sadness stared out the window and came up with an idea. "How about we wake her up?"

"Sadness, that's ridiculous," Joy said. "How could we possibly . . ." She followed Sadness's gaze and saw what she was staring at: Dream Productions. "How about we wake her up!" Joy said.

Joy, Sadness, and Bing Bong hopped off the train and quickly made their way over to Dream Productions. The busy studio was full of action and excitement. Actors in all kinds of costumes walked around sipping coffee and carrying scripts, grips pushed rolling sets, and golf carts zipped from stage to stage.

"Whoa!" said Joy, taking in the scene. "This place is huge."

"Yeah, it looks so much smaller than I expected," Sadness said.

Joy almost fainted when they walked by the star of a majority of Riley's dreams: Rainbow Unicorn. "She's *right there*!" Joy whispered in awe, pointing at the unicorn casually sitting in a director's chair.

Sadness walked right up to her. "My friend says you're famous," she said. "She wants your autograph."

"No, no, Sadness, don't bother Miss Unicorn, okay?" Joy said, grabbing Sadness. "Sorry," she said to the unicorn. "She's from out of town. That was so embarrassing, right?" Joy awkwardly pulled Sadness away. Then she popped her head back toward Rainbow Unicorn and squealed, "I loved you in *Fairy Dream Adventure Part 7*! Okay, bye! I love you!"

Dashing away, Joy caught up with Sadness and Bing Bong. They had reached one of the stages and were just walking right in. The dream director was addressing the cast and crew. "Today's memories are in," the director declared. "We've got a lot to work with here. Riley dumped her best friend, had a miserable day at school, and quit hockey."

Joy, Bing Bong, and Sadness hid behind some production equipment and watched the director pass out scripts. Then they sneaked over to the costume area. "Okay, how are we gonna wake her up?" Joy asked.

"Well, she wakes up sometimes when she has a scary dream. We could scare her," Sadness offered.

Joy didn't like that idea at all. She thought Riley had been through enough and didn't want her to dream of anything that would make her uncomfortable. "Sadness, I know Riley. We're gonna make her so happy that she'll wake up with exhilaration. We'll excite her awake!" said Joy.

"That's never happened before," Sadness said as she watched Joy rummage through the costume racks.

"Ooh, Riley loves dogs," Joy said. "Put this on!" She threw half of a dog costume to Sadness.

"I don't think that'll work," Sadness said, but Joy ignored her and turned to Bing Bong.

"Don't let anything happen to these," she said, handing him the bag of core memories. Bing Bong promised to keep them safe.

The dream director checked the monitor and asked the cameraman to put on the reality distortion filter.

The filter made the phony-looking set and actors look completely real! "Love it," she said, then reminded everyone to play to the camera. "Riley is the camera!" she barked. "Makeup, get out of there, we are on in five, four, three . . ."

The makeup artists finished powdering an actress playing Riley's teacher and the Sleep Lights flashed on. Magical-sounding harp music played, signaling the start of the dream.

Inside Headquarters, Fear was drinking a cup of tea as he sat at the console, watching the dream unfold. He was not happy to be stuck with Dream Duty, but with Joy gone, he had no choice.

"Man, she is one bad actress," Fear said to himself, watching the teacher unenthusiastically talk about a pop quiz. Then the teacher called on Riley to introduce herself. As the camera rose to look like Riley was standing at her desk, one of the students said, "Ew, look! Her teeth are falling out!" Teeth rained down in front of the camera.

"Teeth falling out," Fear said, scoffing. "Let me guess, we have no pants on."

Another student spoke. "Hey, look! She came to school with no pants on!" The camera tilted down, revealing Riley's bare legs.

"Called it!" Fear said.

Joy and Sadness waited off camera at the stage in Dream Productions, wearing the dog costume. "Ready?" Joy whispered.

"I don't think this happy thing is going to work. But if we scare her—" Sadness tried to explain, but Joy didn't let her finish.

"Just . . . follow my lead. Here we go!" Joy yanked Sadness onto the set, dancing and barking like a dog.

The dream director flipped through her script, confused, as she tried to find the current scene. "Who is that?" she whispered to herself.

Joy and Sadness continued to run around in the dog costume, barking, licking students, and acting cute.

Joy looked at the sleep indicator—the needle was still on the Sleep side. She signaled Bing Bong and he released bunches of colorful balloons that poured down onto the classroom set. "Woo!" Joy yelled. "Let's party! Let's dance! Woo!" Then Bing Bong fired a confetti canon and a storm of confetti covered everything!

In Headquarters, Fear perked up. "Hey, a party!" he said, watching the dog happily running around in the balloons and confetti.

"Joy, this isn't working," said Sadness.

Bing Bong danced around offstage and knocked into a light, causing the backdrop to come down. Then the dog costume ripped in half! Joy chased after Sadness on the set. "Sadness, what are you doing? Come back here!"

Fear spit out his tea as he watched the startling sight on-screen: through the reality distortion filter, it looked just like a real dog split right down the middle!

On the screen, it looked as if half a dog were chasing its other half. "It's just a dream, it's just a dream, it's just a dream," Fear chanted, trying to soothe himself. He turned a knob on the console which caused Riley to stir in her sleep.

The dream director watched in horror. "They're trying to wake her up! Call security!" she yelled.

Joy grabbed Sadness's arm and scolded her. "You are ruining this dream! You're scaring her!"

"But look, it's working!" said Sadness, pointing at the sleep indicator. The needle was starting to move toward Awake.

"Whoa!" Joy said.

But before they could do anything else, security entered. The dream director pointed to Bing Bong, Sadness, and Joy. *"They are not part of this dream! Get them!"* she yelled.

Sadness saw the guards and grabbed Joy, pulling her backstage. "Stop right there," a security guard called after them. A second guard got Bing Bong and tackled him to the ground.

"Ow! Hey!" cried Bing Bong.

"Pan away! Pan away!" shouted the director. The camera operator moved the camera away from the disaster happening on set, revealing Rainbow Unicorn eating at the snack table in a mystical unicorn forest set.

Fear shouted at the screen. "Boo! Pick a plot line."

Joy and Sadness watched as the guards dragged Bing Bong, holding the bag of core memories, down toward a massive, scary-looking door.

16

"There go the core memories," Joy whispered to Sadness.

The guards opened the heavy door and a spooky light spilled out along with the frightening sounds of thunder, howling, screaming, roars, and circus music.

"I can't go in there. I'm scared of the dark. Please!" Bing Bong said as they threw him inside. The door slammed shut.

"C'mon," said Joy, grabbing Sadness. They quietly sneaked to the door down a long staircase. "What is this place?" Joy asked.

"The Subconscious," answered Sadness. "I read

about it in the manual. It's where they take all the troublemakers."

Joy and Sadness paused as they watched the guards. They were so busy bickering that Joy and Sadness tiptoed past without them even noticing. Once in front of the door, Sadness shook it, causing the guards to finally see them.

"Hey! You!" said one of the guards.

"Oh! You caught us!" Sadness said sheepishly, acting like she had just come out of the Subconscious.

"Get back in there! No escaping!" said the other guard, as they shoved Joy and Sadness through the doorway.

"Hohhh . . . I don't like it here," Sadness whispered as they walked in cautiously. "It's where they keep Riley's darkest fears."

Joy gasped. "It's broccoli!"

A door eerily creaked open, revealing a dark set of stairs leading down below. Sadness and Joy screamed. "The stairs to the basement!" Sadness exclaimed as they scampered away.

They screamed again as a giant vacuum cleaner started to chase them! "Grandma's vacuum cleaner!" Joy said as they ran and hid behind a rock.

When they decided to walk on, a loud crinkling noise seemed to come from beneath their feet. *Crunch! Crunch!*

"Would you walk quieter?" Joy said, blaming Sadness.

"I'm trying!" Sadness whispered.

Then they noticed a trail of candy wrappers on the floor. They followed the trail into a dark cave. There, on top of a giant mound, was Bing Bong. He was crying inside a cage made out of long, colorful balloons.

"Joy?" Bing Bong said, peering at them in the darkness. He pointed below him and said, "Shhhhhh!"

Joy looked down to see where Bing Bong was pointing—the balloon cage was sitting right on top of a gigantic sleeping clown! "It's Jangles," Joy said, terrified.

Jangles was snoring and talking in his sleep. "Who's the birthday girl?" he muttered.

It gave Joy and Sadness the creeps. They stepped gingerly around the giant clown, and Joy carefully climbed up to get to Bing Bong. "Do you have the core memories?" she whispered when she got close enough.

"Yeah," he said, handing her the bag. "All he cared about was the candy!"

Joy grabbed hold of the cage and tried to pry open the balloon bars. *SQUEEEEEE!* The balloons made a horrible squeaky noise and Jangles stirred. Joy held her breath as the clown fell back asleep. Then she stretched the bars even farther apart and Bing Bong slipped through. They hurried off the creepy clown mountain and rushed toward the exit.

"We're out of here!" said Bing Bong. "Let's get to that train and wait for morning."

Joy slowed down, thinking about what Bing Bong had just said. She couldn't wait until morning to get the core memories back. Joy looked at Jangles and had an idea.

"Oh no," said Bing Bong, watching as Joy and Sadness walked back to the sleeping clown.

They both honked the clown's nose, which caused his wild eyes to pop wide open! Then the massive, creepy Jangles stood up, towering over them.

"H-h-hey, Sadness," Joy said. "Di—did you hear about the p-pahh-party that we're having?"

"Ohh yeah, yes, Joy! Isn't it a ba-bahhh-birthday party?"

"Did you say . . . birthday?" the giant clown asked.

"Yes." Joy struggled to get the words out. "And there's going to be cake, and presents and—"

"—and games and balloons," Sadness added.

"A BIRTHDAY?" screamed Jangles, pulling out his giant mallet and holding it up, ready for birthday action.

"Follow us!" shouted Joy, leading the way.

Jangles laughed a maniacal laugh as he chased Joy, Sadness, and Bing Bong through the door.

"Nothing like a good scare to wake you up, right?" Joy said, looking at Sadness.

Outside the Subconscious, the guards were still arguing when suddenly . . . BASH! Jangles' giant mallet smashed through the front gate. The guards jumped in terror, screaming, "AHHHHHHHHH!"

Joy, Sadness, and Bing Bong were free. They ran up the stairs, leading Jangles toward Dream Productions.

Inside Headquarters, Fear had nearly fallen asleep watching the boring unicorn dream when . . . BLAM! The creepy clown came crashing through the set! "WHO'S THE BIRTHDAY GIRL?" Jangles' voice boomed across the stage.

Fear screamed. He smacked his hand down on the button to wake Riley up, and then he passed out!

Riley bolted up in bed, waking from the nightmare. The sign in Dream Productions read AWAKE.

17

Joy, Sadness, and Bing Bong rushed off the stage of Riley's dream at Dream Productions, leaving Jangles behind as he smashed up the sets and everything in his path with his giant mallet. They hurried toward the Train of Thought.

The train was moving! The three leapt aboard the very last car.

"Ha ha!" Joy said. "We made it!" They laughed and celebrated. She grabbed Sadness and swung her around. "Guess who's on their way to Headquarters?" Joy sang.

"We are!" said Sadness.

Back at Headquarters, Anger and Disgust stumbled out of the break room, disheveled and barely awake. "What is going on?" asked Disgust.

"He did it again," said Anger, gesturing to Fear trembling beneath the console.

"We were at school, and we were naked, and there was a dog, and his back half was chasing him . . . ," Fear rambled, recalling Riley's dream.

Anger was reaching his limit. "It was a DREAM! This is ridiculous, we can't even get a good night's sleep anymore. Time to take action."

Anger stomped off and retrieved the idea he had held up earlier. He stood at the console, ready to plug it in. "Who's with me?" He looked at Fear, who was still recovering and unable to utter a word. Then he looked at Disgust and waited for a response.

"Yeah, let's do it," said Disgust finally.

Anger plugged the lightbulb-shaped idea into the console.

Inside her bedroom, Riley's expression changed. She pulled out her laptop.

"She took it. There's no turning back," said Anger.

"So, how're we gonna get to Minnesota from here?" Disgust asked.

"Well, why don't we go to the elephant lot and rent an elephant?" Anger asked sarcastically. Then he yelled, "We're taking the bus!"

Riley pulled up the Greyhound bus website and began to look at the schedule for buses to Minnesota.

"A ticket costs money," said Disgust. "How do we get money?"

"Mom's purse," Anger said casually.

Disgust gasped. "You wouldn't."

"Oh, but I would," said Anger. "Where was it we saw it last?"

He punched up a memory and the Tripledent singers came on again, singing the theme song.

"NOOOO!" Anger slammed down on the console, ejecting the memory. Then he remembered that Mom's purse was downstairs somewhere. "Mom and Dad got us into this mess," Anger said. "They can pay to get us out."

Inside the train, Joy, Bing Bong, and Sadness were happily speeding along. Joy looked at Sadness. "Hey, that was a good idea," she said. "About scaring Riley awake."

"Really?" Sadness said, sounding surprised.

"Nice work."

Sadness brightened a little as Joy exhaled, feeling

relieved. "I can't wait to get the old Riley back," she said. "As soon as we get there, I'm going to fix this whole mess."

Bing Bong had found a box of memories and was looking through them. He discovered a recent memory and saw that Riley was much older than he had thought. "Whoa," he said. "Is this Riley?"

Joy took the memory to get a closer look. She nodded.

"She's so big now," Bing Bong said. "She won't fit in my rocket. How're we gonna get to the moon?"

Joy recognized the memory. "Oh, it's that time in the twisty tree, remember? The hockey team showed up and Mom and Dad were there cheering . . . Look at her, having fun and laughing. It's my favorite." Joy sat back down, beside Sadness.

"I love that one, too," said Sadness.

Joy couldn't believe it! Sadness actually liked a happy memory. "Atta girl!" she said. "Now you're getting it!"

Sadness stared at the memory. "Yeah," she said, remembering. "It was the day the Prairie Dogs lost the big playoff game. Riley missed the winning shot. She felt awful. She wanted to quit."

Joy's face fell. Sadness had started out so positive.

"Sorry," Sadness apologized. "I went sad again, didn't I?"

"I'll tell you what," Joy said. "We'll keep working on that when we get back. Okay?"

Sadness smiled. "Okay."

Meanwhile, Riley sneaked downstairs to find her mom's purse. Mom was in the kitchen on the phone, talking to the moving company, so Riley was able to find the purse and slip the credit card out quietly. She put it in her pocket and crept back upstairs without Mom noticing.

Joy looked wistfully out the train window. All of a sudden a loud BOOM broke the spell. "Honesty Island!" Joy shrieked.

The train tracks they were on began to sway as Honesty Island started to collapse below them. Joy, Sadness, and Bing Bong were jostled back and forth. Screaming, they fell as the train started to tumble, the tracks slipping away with the collapsing island.

The train crashed onto the side of a cliff and began to tip over as mind workers rushed on board.

"Let's *go*! Move it! Move it!" the workers shouted, trying to get everyone off safely.

Joy, Sadness, and Bing Bong jumped to land just in time as the train plummeted into the Memory Dump below. Joy couldn't believe it. "That was our way home!" she said. "We lost another island. . . . What is happening?"

"Haven't you heard?" asked a worker. "Riley is running away."

18

In her quiet, empty bedroom, Riley pulled her books out of her backpack and picked up her clothes, ready to pack them in her bag. Then she paused and her expression changed.

Fear was driving. "Are we really doing this? I mean, this is serious," he said.

Anger pushed Fear aside and took control. "Look," he said. "We have no core memories. You want Riley to be happy? Let's get back to Minnesota and make some."

Riley's worried expression faded and was replaced with anger as she stuffed her clothes into her bag and exited the room.

Out on the cliff, Sadness, Joy, and Bing Bong stared at the empty space where Honesty Island used to be.

"Joy, if we hurry, we can still stop her," said Sadness, offering a ray of hope.

There was only one island left . . . and one lightline that they could follow back to Headquarters. "Family Island," said Joy. "Let's go!"

They ran along the cliff edge, bolting toward the bridge to Family Island. Sadness saw the island start to quake and yelled, "It's too dangerous! We won't make it in time!"

Joy looked out to see pieces of Family Island falling away. "But that's our only way back!"

The shaking island had caused parts of Long-Term Memory to collapse and break apart. Suddenly, Sadness pointed over to a memory recall tube. The tubes were normally buried deep beneath the shelving of Long-Term Memory, but with all the earthquake-like movement, one of them had become exposed. If they got to it in time, maybe they could get sucked up and sent back to Headquarters.

"A recall tube!" said Joy.

"We can get recalled!" Sadness added.

They ran past the bridge and headed for the tube.

With her bag strapped to her back, Riley walked toward the front door of the house. "Have a great day, sweetheart," Mom called from the kitchen.

"See you after school, monkey," Dad added, making monkey noises.

"We love you!" Mom said.

Riley didn't respond. She just turned and walked right out the front door, headed for the bus station.

Joy, Sadness, and Bing Bong were closing in on the tube, but Family Island quaked and twisted the bridge like a piece of taffy. Then a large piece of the island broke off!

"Go!" shouted Joy. "Run, *run*!" A nearby cliff cracked and crashed down into the dump, and the ridge where they were just standing fell away. They screamed as they fled the crumbling chunks of land and headed toward the recall tube.

Joy stepped into the lower section of the recall tube first, with Sadness right behind her. But the tube was small and there wasn't enough room.

Sadness and Joy jostled against each other and the memories inside the bag started to change color. "Whoa, whoa! Sadness!" Joy cautioned. The bag emitted a blue light, and Joy tried to push Sadness away. "Sadness, stop! You're hurting Riley!" Joy pulled one of the memories out of the bag. It was bright blue. Sadness stepped back, horrified.

"Oh no!" she said. "I did it again!"

"If you get in here, these core memories will be sad," Joy said.

RUMBLE! Joy looked to see the source of the terrible sound: the family statue on Family Island was breaking apart. Joy didn't know what to do! She had to make a quick decision. "I'm sorry . . . Riley needs to be happy."

Joy pulled the tube closed and began to ride it up

to Headquarters . . . alone.

"Joy?" Sadness called after her friend as she stood with Bing Bong on the cliff.

Then the intense rumbling from below made the cliffside fall and shook the tube apart. Joy fell from the tube. Bing Bong reached for her, but the ground beneath him disintegrated, causing them both to fall into the abyss.

"Joy!" Sadness cried. Feeling helpless as she stood on the cliff's edge, she buried her face in her hands.

Joy landed with a *thud* and groaned as she rolled down the long, steep hill into the shadows filled with faded memories. When she finally stopped, she looked around, confused, trying to figure out where she was.

She hugged the bag of core memories tightly. All the memories were still inside.

Then she looked up at the ledge high above her. Suddenly, she knew where she was: the Memory Dump! She couldn't believe how far she had fallen. She frantically ran up the steep mountain, trying to climb it, but came crashing back down. She tried again and again, but each time she tumbled right back down to the bottom.

A short distance away, Bing Bong was looking down at his hand: it was beginning to fade. "Oh no," he said. He ran off to find Joy.

When he finally reached her, Joy was still trying to claw her way up the mountain.

"Joy, what are you doing?" Bing Bong asked. "Would you stop, please?"

But Joy ignored him and continued trying to scale the cliff.

"Don't you get it, Joy? We're stuck down here. We're forgotten."

Joy stopped in her tracks, feeling the pain of Bing Bong's words. She looked down at her feet and watched as the memories around her faded and disappeared. A short distance away lay the blue core memory of Riley crying in class. Her heart breaking, Joy fell to her knees as tears began to run down her face.

She tried to focus on the old happy memories of young Riley. "Remember how she used to stick her tongue out when she was coloring?" Joy said longingly.

She continued to flip through old memories, watching and remembering happier times. "I could listen to her stories all day," she said, watching one of three-year-old Riley talking to a bug.

Joy finally picked up the blue core memory. She couldn't believe how miserable Riley was. "I just wanted Riley to be happy, and now . . ." Feeling truly hopeless, Joy cried even harder.

One of Joy's tears fell onto the sphere that contained the faded memory of the twisty tree. Joy wiped the tear away and it accidentally rewound the memory . . . and the color of the sphere changed from gold to blue.

In the memory, Riley sat in the tree with her parents as the team approached in the distance. Joy looked closer and closer. Then she used her hand to rewind the memory farther. She remembered what Sadness had said: *It was the day the Prairie Dogs lost the big playoff game. Riley missed the winning shot. She felt awful. She wanted to quit.*

Joy watched as the hockey team surrounded Riley in the twisty tree, and suddenly she realized . . .

Mom and Dad . . . the team . . . they had come to help because of Sadness.

Joy turned to Bing Bong with renewed energy. She knew what had to be done. "We have to get back up there," she said, determined.

Bing Bong looked at her sadly. "Joy, we're stuck down here forever. We might as well be on another planet."

"Another planet," Joy said thoughtfully. That gave her an idea—what about taking Bing Bong's rocket ship to the moon? She started to sing his theme song.

Bing Bong's eyes lit up as he understood the plan, and he joined her in song. As the melody drifted across the dump, off in the distance Bing Bong's rocket answered back by *bing*ing and *bong*ing!

Joy and Bing Bong ran toward the sound and found the rocket. They could fly out of the dump!

They pulled the rocket wagon up one of the big mountains. "Hop in!" Joy shouted, and they both climbed inside. Bing Bong pushed off and they sang their hearts out. The song powered the rocket as it sped down the mountain. When it reached the bottom, it shot up the next hill, launching into the air.

Joy reached for the high ledge above the dump . . . but they weren't even close. They crashed back down. "C'mon!" Joy said, ready to try again.

They took the wagon up another mountain, singing even louder now. But again they fell short of the ledge and dropped back into the dump. The rocket just didn't have enough power. Bing Bong looked down at his hand and noticed that it was disappearing!

"Come on, Joy," he said, reaching out to help her stand. "One more time. I've got a feeling about this one."

They took the wagon up the mountain and sang once again. "Louder!" yelled Bing Bong. "Louder, Joy! Sing louder!"

When they reached the base of the mountain, Bing Bong dove out of the wagon, but Joy didn't notice. Without his additional weight, the wagon had plenty of momentum. Bing Bong watched as Joy and the wagon soared into the air.

"We're going to make it!" Joy shouted as she flew closer and closer to the ledge.

The rocket made it! "Woo-hoo!" Joy cried. "Bing Bong, we did it! We—" Joy turned around and gasped. "Bing Bong? Bing Bong!"

Joy hurried to the edge and looked over the side. Bing Bong was down at the bottom, laughing and dancing. "Ya ha ha!" he sang. "You made it! Ha ha! Go! Go save Riley! Ha ha ha! Take her to the moon for me. Okay?" Bing Bong waved and vanished.

"I'll try, Bing Bong," Joy said, hanging her head. "I promise."

20

When Riley's parents came home, they were surprised to find that she wasn't there. "I'll call her cell," said Mom.

Riley's cell phone rang as she walked through the streets of San Francisco. She looked down at who was calling.

"It's Mom. She's on to us. Where's my bag?" asked Fear, looking for his paper bag. He felt as if he was about to hyperventilate.

"What do we do?" asked Disgust.

"Riley needs to get core memories. We keep going," said Anger.

Riley ignored the call, put the phone in her pocket, and continued to walk toward the bus station.

Joy frantically ran through the aisles of Long-Term Memory, searching for Sadness as Family Island began to break apart behind her. "C'mon, Sadness, where are you? Okay. If I was Sadness, where would I be?" Joy looked around and imagined being Sadness. "Ohhh . . . everything is awful and my legs don't work and you have to drag me around while I touch all the—" Joy said, imitating her. She slumped to the ground and kicked her leg up in the air. Then she saw something: a trail of blue memories on the bottom shelves! Joy followed the trail.

Meanwhile, Riley had made it to the station and was standing in line to get on the bus. Her cell phone rang. It was Mom again. Her phone read "15 missed calls from Mom."

"Oh . . . it's Mom again," said Fear. "What do we do?" He began to breathe faster into his bag.

BOOM! Family Island rumbled behind them. It was the only island still standing.

"This is madness! She shouldn't run away," said Anger.

"Let's get this idea out of her head," said Disgust.

Fear and Anger agreed, and the three rushed to the console to unplug the idea.

Joy was still searching for Sadness in Long Term Memory, following the trail of blue memories. "Sadness!" she called.

Sadness turned around. "Joy?" She was surprised to see her, but she couldn't face her. She ran away.

"Wait!" shouted Joy.

"Just let me go," Sadness called, still running. "Riley's better off without me!"

Joy chased Sadness into Imagination Land. Sadness toppled fries from French Fry Forest into Joy's path to slow her down.

"Come back!" yelled Joy. Then she used a super-long fry to pole vault over the mound of fallen fries.

She tried to follow close behind Sadness but lost her in Cloud Town. Suddenly, a shadow passed over Joy, causing her to look up. Sadness was flying overhead on a chunk of cloud, away from Headquarters. "What? Sadness!" Joy called.

"I only make everything worse," Sadness cried as she drifted farther away.

"Wait—Sadness! We've gotta get you back to . . ." Joy chased after her, but the cloud was moving too fast.

Joy didn't know how she was going to catch up with Sadness until suddenly, her eyes fell on the Imaginary Boyfriend Generator.

Inside Headquarters, Anger struggled as he tried to untwist the idea bulb from the console. "It's stuck!" he shouted.

"Oh, great," said Disgust.

"Whaddaya mean it's stuck?" said Fear, reaching out to try.

"Now what?" asked Disgust.

Then the console started to shut down! A strange blackness slowly crept across the console, like a dark, scary blob. "What is *this*?" cried Fear. Nobody knew.

Riley stepped onto the bus.

Thinking the idea bulb was making the console shut down, Fear struggled with it, but it wouldn't budge. He even tried using a crowbar. As Fear strained to pry it out, he lost control and the crowbar whacked him in the face.

"Make her feel scared!" urged Disgust. "That'll make her change her mind!"

Fear frantically pushed buttons and pulled levers on the mostly black console, but nothing worked.

"Guys," he said, turning his gaze to Disgust and Anger. "We can't make Riley feel anything."

21

Joy ran up to the Imaginary Boyfriend Generator.

"Hey!" she said, addressing the Imaginary Boyfriend, who sat slowly plucking petals off a flower. "Did you mean what you said before?"

"I would die for Riley! I would die for Riley! I would die—" the boyfriend replied.

"Yeah, yeah, okay, Haircut," Joy said. "Time to prove it."

Joy scooped up the Imaginary Boyfriend and put him in the bag she had gotten from Bing Bong. Then she turned on the generator and a bunch of imaginary boyfriends began to pour out. They moved down the conveyor belt, shouting, "I would die for Riley!" Joy caught each one in the imaginary bag.

"That's good," she said, putting the last boyfriend in.

As Sadness floated up ahead on her cloud, Joy ran past her and yanked on a twisty palm tree made from balloons, pulling it from the ground. With careful aim, she untied it and used the rush of air from the balloons to blow Sadness and her cloud back toward the Memory Dump.

Joy sped up, running along the cliff's edge, parallel to Sadness, as they both moved closer to Family Island. Joy finally stopped, her eyes on Sadness, and aligned herself with Family Island. All of a sudden, Joy dumped the bag and the boyfriends poured out. Their momentum pulled Joy to the top of an incredibly tall tower of imaginary boyfriends.

"This is crazy," Joy said to herself. "No! Be positive." She took a deep breath. "I am *positive* this is crazy."

The tower of teen boys swayed as Joy gazed at Headquarters in the distance. She looked out at the trampoline on Family Island, then back at Sadness, and calculated her strategy. "NOW!" she shouted.

On Joy's command, the boyfriends took out their

cell phones to take a photo, tipping them forward and launching Joy onto the trampoline. She bounced off and ricocheted into the air, flying toward Sadness. Then she grabbed Sadness midair and carried her along!

"Joy?" asked Sadness, stunned.

"Hang on!" shouted Joy as they soared through the air like birds.

SPLAT! Bull's-eye! The two hit the back window of Headquarters!

The other Emotions ran over. "It's Joy!" exclaimed Disgust.

Fear, Anger, and Disgust tried to open the window but it wouldn't budge.

"Stand back!" shouted Anger. He threw a chair, but it bounced right off.

"That worked," said Disgust.

"Well, what would you do, if you're so smart?" Anger said, annoyed.

Disgust's eyes lit up with an idea. "I'd tell you . . . but you're too dumb to understand," she said.

"What?" Anger asked.

"Of course your tiny brain is confused," Disgust went on, mocking Anger as she tried to get a rise out of him. "Guess I'll have to dumb it down to your level."

Anger let out a giant, angry roar and flames came out of his head. "AAAAAAAAHHHHHHHHH!"

Disgust, who had quickly put on a welding mask, picked him up and used his head like a blowtorch, cutting a hole in the window. They pulled Joy and Sadness up from the ledge and back into Headquarters.

The others were so relieved to see them. "Thank goodness you're back, Joy!" said Fear. "We were just trying to make more happy memories. That's all we wanted to do."

Joy looked at the screen, watching as the bus driver shut the door and pulled away from the station.

"Joy, you've got to fix this," Disgust demanded. "Get up there."

Joy turned and looked at Sadness. "Sadness, it's up to you."

"What?" the others said in unison. "Sadness?!"

Joy hushed them and gave Sadness a look of encouragement.

"Oh . . . I can't, Joy."

Joy pushed Sadness toward the console. "Riley needs you."

"Okay," Sadness said nervously. She took a deep breath and set her hands down on the console. The blackness receded and the idea bulb flickered off. Sadness gently pulled it out as Joy, Anger, Fear, and Disgust watched in amazement.

Inside the bus, Riley's expression changed from listless to sad. Then she stood up, gripping the seat in front of her. "Wait! Stop!" she shouted. The bus stopped and Riley marched up to the front. "I want to get off."

She got off the bus and ran toward home.

22

Riley's parents were worried sick as they racked their brains trying to figure out where she might be. "Her teacher hasn't even seen Riley all day," said Mom.

"I can't believe this," Dad said.

"What was she wearing last? Do you even remember what—" asked Mom, panicking.

Just then, Riley walked through the front door. "Riley!" shouted Mom, rushing to her.

"Riley, there you are! Thank goodness!" said Dad, relieved.

Inside Headquarters, Sadness was confidently driving. Joy pulled the yellow core memories out of the bag and handed them over to her. The memories all turned blue.

In the dining room, Riley cried as Sadness placed each memory, one at a time, into the recall unit. All the memories turned a deeper shade of blue. Sadness continued to work the console, helping Riley as she talked to her parents.

"I know you don't want me to, but . . . I miss home," Riley said through her tears. "I miss Minnesota."

Mom and Dad listened as Riley went on.

"You need me to be happy, but I want my old friends, and my hockey team. . . . I wanna go home. Please don't be mad."

Her parents hugged her. "Oh, sweetie," said Mom.

"We're not mad," said Dad. "You know what? I miss Minnesota, too."

Her parents talked about all the things they missed about Minnesota—the woods, their backyard, the lake. The three of them hugged as Riley continued to sob.

Joy gave Sadness the blue core memory. Sadness took Joy's hand and led her to the controls, placing Joy's hand on the console alongside her own.

The Emotions watched on the screen as Riley smiled through her tears and her parents hugged her tightly.

Joy and Sadness, standing side by side at the console, shared a smile. They were a team. A sudden DING sounded throughout Headquarters as a new core memory was made. This one was gold and blue swirled together . . . a first. Joy and Sadness placed it in the core memory holder and watched as a new Family Island arose, bigger and better than the last.

23

Days later, Riley's Mind World looked very different. Headquarters was getting a major upgrade. While mind workers adjusted the console, the Emotions looked out the window, admiring the new Islands of Personality.

"Hey, I'm liking this view," Fear said.

"Friendship Island has expanded," Anger said. "Glad they finally opened that Friendly Argument section."

"I like Tragic Vampire Romance Island," added Sadness.

"Boy Band Island. Hope that's just a phase," Fear

said, wringing his hands nervously.

"Say what you want—I think it's all beautiful," said Joy, just grateful that there were islands once again.

"All right," one of the workers announced, clearing his throat. "There you go. Your new, expanded console is up and running." The worker hit a button and the shiny new console lit up as the Emotions gazed at it in awe.

Disgust eyed one of the new buttons. "Hey, guys? What's 'pu-ber-ty'?" she asked, reading the word on the button.

Fear and Sadness shrugged as Anger checked out some new additions. "Whoa," he said. "I have access to the entire curse word library!"

On the screen, they could see that Riley and her parents were just getting to the hockey rink. Once inside, Riley's parents gave her some words of wisdom before the game. "Now, when you get out there, you be aggressive!" Dad said.

"I know, Dad," said Riley.

"But not too aggressive," added Mom.

"You know, you guys don't have to come to every game," said Riley. Her parents' faces were completely painted with the team colors.

"Are you kidding? I'm not missing one! Go, Foghorns!" Dad said, making a foghorn noise.

"Go, Riley! Foghorns are the best!" shouted Mom, making a foghorn noise, too.

Riley shushed them. "Okay, okay. I gotta go." She smiled and walked away, feeling a little embarrassed.

Inside Headquarters, Joy was beaming. "Awwww," she said.

"They love us!" Fear exclaimed.

"Yeah, Mom and Dad are pretty cool," said Anger.

"Guys, of course they are," said Disgust, cautioning them. "But we can't *show* it!" She stepped up to the console and pushed a lever.

Inside Dad's head, his Emotions had their faces painted, too! They cheered. "She loved the face painting!" said Dad's Fear happily.

"Ha!" said Dad's Anger. "Told you it was a great idea." Dad turned to Mom and smiled. She smiled back.

Inside Mom's mind, *her* Emotions also had their faces painted! "Best idea he's had in a while," Mom's Anger said.

"He's a really good guy," said Mom's Sadness.

Riley walked toward the ice and accidentally bumped into a teenage boy, causing him to drop his drink. She picked it up and handed it to him. "Sorry," she said, smiling.

Inside the boy's mind, a warning light was BLARING. All of *his* Emotions ran around his Headquarters in a panic. They were yelling at the same time as an alarm sounded: "Girl. Girl. Girl."

The boy stood, stunned, unable to utter a word.

"Uhh . . . Ooooooo-kay," said Riley. She walked away but looked over her shoulder and gave him one last little smile.

"All set, Riley?" asked one of her teammates as she skated onto the ice. Riley high-fived her and they skated into position.

Mom and Dad cheered like crazy from the stands as the game began.

Inside Headquarters, Joy and Sadness stood together at the new console. "All right. Let's play some hockey!" said Joy.

As soon as the puck dropped onto the ice, Riley snapped into action, skating like a pro, with a smile on her face.

"All right, Anger, take it," said Joy.

"Give us that puck or you're dead meat!" shouted Anger.

"On our left! On our left!" screamed Fear.

"Let's just try not to get all smelly this time," Disgust warned.

Joy felt terrific. Riley had made great new friends, was doing well at school, and loved her new hockey team. Things couldn't be better. Joy was confident that she and Sadness, along with the rest of the Emotions, would work together to help Riley live a happy life. Things might have gotten turned inside out and even upside down and around, but everything was going to be just fine.

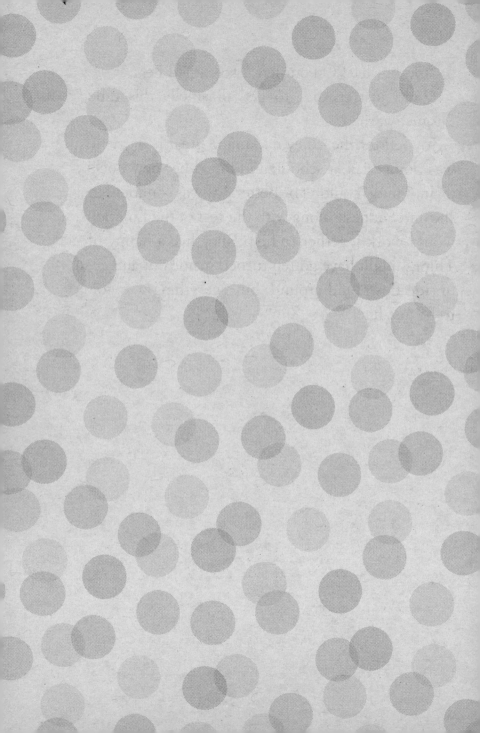